Penelope and the Monsters

written by
Sheri Radford

illustrated by
Christine Tripp

Lobster Press ™

Published by:
Lobster Press™
1620 Sherbrooke Street West, Suites C & D
Montréal, Québec   H3H 1C9
Tel. (514) 904-1100 • Fax (514) 904-1101
www.lobsterpress.com

Publisher: Alison Fripp
Editors: Alison Fripp & Karen Li
Editorial Assistant: Stephanie Normandin
Graphic Design & Production: Tammy Desnoyers

We acknowledge the financial support of the Government
of Canada through the Book Publishing Industry
Development Program (BPIDP) for our publishing activities.

We acknowledge the support of
the Canada Council for the Arts
for our publishing program.

Library and Archives Canada Cataloguing in Publication

Radford, Sheri, 1971-
        Penelope and the monsters / Sheri Radford ; illustrated by Christine Tripp.

(The Penelope series)
ISBN 1-894222-94-6

        I. Tripp, Christine II. Title. III. Series: Radford, Sheri, 1971- . Penelope series.

PS8585.A282P453 2005   jC813'.6   C2004-905459-7

Printed and bound in China.

To Paul, for scaring
away the monsters.

– *Sheri Radford*

For my own 5 monsters:
Eric, Emily, Erin, Elizabeth, and
their father, Donald.

– *Christine Tripp*

"I'm never, ever, not in a million trillion gazillion years going to sleep," Penelope announced to her father as he tucked her into bed.

"You're going to be awfully tired if you stay up that long," her father said.

"But there are monsters in here."

"I don't see any monsters."

"That's because they're hiding. They only come out after you leave," Penelope explained.

"There are no such things as monsters.
Now go to sleep." Penelope's father turned out the
light and shut the door behind him.

Penelope looked around the dark room nervously.
Suddenly, her dresser drawers
started to bang.

She pulled her quilt
up over her chin.
"If there are any
monsters in there,
you can just go
away right now,"
she gulped.

"No monsters here,"
said a tiny voice from inside the drawer.

"We're not monsters. We're gnomes,"
said another tiny voice.

"Shhhhh. We don't want *her* to know that," said a third tiny voice.

"Aaaaahhhhh!" screamed Penelope.

Penelope's father came running into the
room and turned on the light.

"What? What is it?" he cried.

"There are gnomes in my dresser!"
shrieked Penelope.

Penelope's father walked over
to the dresser. He opened each drawer
and looked inside. "Nope," he said. "No gnomes."

"Of course not," said Penelope.
"They only come out after you leave."

"Go to sleep," her father said.

"I'm never, ever, not in a million trillion gazillion years
going to sleep," Penelope said.

Penelope's father turned out the light and closed the door.

As soon as he was gone, the doors to Penelope's closet started to rattle.

Penelope pulled her quilt up over her nose. "If there are any monsters in there, you can just go away right now," she gulped.

"No monsters here," said a medium-sized voice from inside the closet.

"We're not monsters. We're trolls," said another medium-sized voice.

"Shhhhh. We don't want *her* to know that," said a third medium-sized voice.

"Aaaaahhhhh!" screamed Penelope.

Penelope's father opened the door and turned on the light.

"What? What is it now?" he asked.

"There are trolls in my closet!" shrieked Penelope.

Penelope's father sighed and opened the closet doors.
"Look. No trolls."

"Of course not," said Penelope.
"They only come out after you leave."

"Go to sleep,"
her father said.

"I'm never, ever, not in
a million trillion gazillion
years going to sleep,"
Penelope said.

Penelope's father turned
out the light and closed
the door.

As soon as he was gone, Penelope's bed started to shake.

Penelope pulled her quilt up over her eyes. "If there are any monsters under there, you can just go away right now," she gulped.

"No monsters here,"
said a very large voice.

"We're not monsters. We're giants,"
said another very large voice.

"Shhhhh. We don't want *her* to know that,"
said a third very large voice.

"Aaaaahhhhh!"
screamed Penelope.

"Go to sleep!" Penelope's father yelled from down the hall.

"I'm never, ever, not in a million trillion gazillion years going to sleep," Penelope yelled back. She pulled her quilt up over her head.

Penelope's bed kept shaking.
Penelope stayed under her quilt.

The dresser drawers started to bang.
Penelope stayed under her quilt.

The closet doors started to rattle.
Penelope stayed under her quilt.

Her teeth chattered, her knees clattered, her heart
fluttered and thumped. She shivered and quivered.
She trembled and quaked. But the shaking and
banging and rattling went
on and on...

and on and on and
on and on and on
and on...

and on and on and
on and on and on and
on and on...

and on and on and on
and on and on and on
and on and on...

and on and on...

"Enough!" Penelope shouted,
throwing off her quilt and turning on the light.

"Hey, all you monsters!
Why don't you stop hiding if you're so scary?
Why don't you come out and scare me?"

Nothing happened.

"If you want to scare me,
you'll have to come
out and do it now,"
said Penelope.

Nothing happened.

"I'm waiting," said
Penelope.

TAP TAP
TAP TAP

The dresser drawers opened, and three tiny gnomes hopped out.

Three medium-sized trolls jumped out of the closet.

Three very large giants crawled out from under the bed.

They all stared at Penelope.

Penelope stared back at them.

"You're not very scary at all," said Penelope.

The gnomes and trolls and giants all looked disappointed.

"You're actually pretty silly-looking," said Penelope.

The gnomes and trolls and giants all looked insulted.

"In fact," added Penelope, "my father says you don't even *exist*."

"What?"

The gnomes and trolls and giants all looked furious.
They turned their backs on Penelope and held
a secret meeting.

Then, without even saying goodbye, they all walked
out her bedroom door.

Penelope turned off the light and crawled into bed.
She smiled to herself.

"I'm never, ever, not in a million trillion gazillion years
going to be afraid of monsters again," she said.

The next night, Penelope's father's dresser drawers started to bang.

(No monsters in there.
But, *shhh*, we don't
want *him* to know
that!)